TALKING HANDS

Janine Scott

Photography by
Siân Bradfield

Hi! My name is Angelos.
I am deaf.
I cannot hear what
other people say.

I use sign language.
I talk with my hands.
I have name signs for my friends and my family.

Here is Tom.
He is my friend from school.
Tom likes to read in the library.

Here is my name sign for Tom.
It means "book".
BOOK

Here is Molly.
She is my friend from school, too.
Molly has a pet turtle.
She takes very good care of it.

My name sign for Molly is “turtle”.

Here is my friend Ella.
She lives next door to me.
Ella loves to surf in the ocean.

My name sign for Ella is “surfing”.

Here is my friend Luke.
We have been friends for a long time.
Luke collects helicopters.
He wants to fly one when he is older.

My name sign for Luke is "helicopter".
HELICOPTER

Here is my little brother, Kris.
Kris loves his teddy bear.
He takes it everywhere.

My name sign for Kris is "teddy".
TEDDY

I like kangaroos.
Can you guess my name sign?

It is “kangaroo”.
I can hop like a kangaroo, too!

SIGN INDEX